The Trumpet Fisherman

and other Istanbul Sketches

New stories by

James Tressler

The Trumpet Fisherman and other Istanbul Sketches

by James Tressler

Sky Blue Press, 2012

Contents

Istanbul is a network of villages woven, one might even say, thrown together, rather than a single vast city. It is a city that defies perspective, for it is constantly shifting. It is an intricate mosaic, the individual pieces of the mosaic giving meaning and substance to the whole.

"Muses never talk among themselves; each one works in their own domain, and when they aren't working, they dance."
-- Degas

Evening in Kadıköy

In the days of the Ottoman Empire, the streets of Istanbul were plagued by dogs (in some parts of the city this hasn't changed to this day); street dogs who wandered alone and, at night, in packs. They were generally well taken care of; any dog that lingered outside the door of a café would be given some morsel from the kitchen.

In Kadiköy what strikes you immediately are not dogs, but cats. You rarely see roaming dogs in this sea-side district on Istanbul 's Asian side, but there are cats aplenty. In the evenings after the fish markets close, the pavements freshly sprayed, the metal doors pulled down, the cats will congregate, peering, sniffing, and licking the last traces of the fish sold that day.

Kadiköy is like that; a visitor, too, finds himself, like those cats, lurking in the street, at twilight, roaming, waiting for something or someone to materialize in the dusk, exactly who or what you don't know. Anyway, there is that anticipation, that eagerness, that regret, lingering like the phosphorous gleam on the skin of passing faces: Kadiköy, a cat looking for fish in the dusk.

The men who sit in door ways of barber shops, or watering down the fish in the markets to keep them fresh, or the grocers presiding over vegetables reposing in the lingering heat; the endless stream of taxis and buses and *dolmuş*, honking desperately against the congested, humid air; the muezzin marking the end of the day, releasing a prayer over the yawls of overheated felines, over the mocking warble of sea birds.

It is at the waterfront where you finally find release. Here on the waterfront, the churning waters of the Bosphorous, looking out toward the Sea of Marmara , where ships dot the horizon, people sit and order fish sandwiches and lemonade or tea while the ferries from the European side come in and out. A gentle evening breeze lifts your gaze outward, past the minarets of the Aya Sofia and Sultanahmet mosques, and out toward the final release of the sea.

For the eternally restless or whimsical heart, Kadiköy can seem a notch down from Taksim, the entertainment hub over on the European side. But it's not without its charms. There is the Bosphorous, a cradle rocking back and forth between two continents, the assurance of escape the sea offers, the markets and their endless goods. The women, in mostly modern dress, but with some women wearing headscarves here and there, sit at the cafes, their skin glowing with faint perspiration in the fragrant air. The street musicians, as well as those in the cafes, offer an endlessly syncopated, melismatic counterpoint to the warm evenings. Beneath canopies of cool ivy, people sit at café tables drinking Efes beer or rakı, a kind of Turkish absinthe, and talking, playing backgammon or watching football (Fenerbahçe is the local favorite, the stadium just ten minutes away).

Up the hill from the market, through a maze of streets, is what is colloquially known as “Bar Street ,” for anyone looking to get in a pub crawl. Bar Street is exactly that, a slender avenue packed with indoor and outdoor pubs. A night out drinking in Istanbul isn’t cheap, though not outlandish either; generally, though it is just as well to stick to the cafes near the market, for the prices are about the same, but generally there is more live music.

Anyway, Kadiköy sways to a slightly different rhythm than its rivals across the Bosphorous – riotous, noisy Taksim, atmospheric Galata with its stone tower gazing out proudly at the beginning of the Muslim world; steep, commercial Beyoğlu. There’s less foot traffic, a detached, slightly provincial aesthetic, fewer tourists.

Speaking of cats; I’m thinking of Burcu. That’s not her real name, just one that I’ve randomly given her. In our building there is a kind of no-man’s land that I can see outside my bedroom window. An expanse of overgrown bushes, trash and unfinished-looking walls serves instead of a courtyard and connects the other buildings. From the window you look out and see the other apartments, with laundry hung out to dry on the balconies. Also from the windows, looking down into the no-man’s land, you see cats. I’ve never counted them but there are at least a half dozen, most of them caramel-colored, dingy and wild. High above on the tops of the buildings are sea birds with their grisly, mocking laughter.

Because of the heat it's best to keep the windows open. It was because of this that I met Burcu. She was a calico cat, with wide green eyes that I discovered in my room one evening. As soon as I entered, she popped back out the window, her calico tail swishing as she disappeared. I didn't like the idea at all of one of these neighborhood cats hanging out in my room, so I was quick to discourage her any time she got near the window. Then one day she went into heat, and her yowling, wandering and hovering became intolerable. It was a hot Sunday afternoon, I had the windows open and was reading in bed. Then I saw her nose poking in the room. Incensed, I got up; she darted back, but remained on the sill. Moved by a sudden evil impulse, I picked her up and flicked her (she had just enough time to utter a shriek of surprise) down into the no-man's land. She fell, turning over in the air, and landed in a bush.

I watched to see if Burcu would be able to climb back up. For several minutes, she peered and sniffed around, disoriented, looking up at me in feline surprise. Pitilessly, I enjoyed being a spectator to her predicament. I forgot my reading and waited to see what would happen. She found a barred window, crawled through it and disappeared into a dark area. Just then, three or four cats, the caramel-colored ones, having scented Burcu, came prancing from hidden places and assumed positions near the window. One of them, the biggest, went into the dark area and for a few minutes it was quiet. Then suddenly there was a shriek and Burcu came bounding out the window, streaking past, followed closely by her new admirer.

A stand-off then ensued; it went on for the next several hours. The big cat would make an advance, Burcu would hiss and shriek and swipe her claws at him, then run, pursued by the other cats.

Later, when it got dark I was watching football with my flat mate, Osman. I mentioned the afternoon's drama. As he listened to my description of the cat, Osman suddenly started. "That wasn't a street cat," he said. "That was our neighbor's cat!"

The neighbor, it seemed, was out of town that weekend. Osman, who was studying to be a vet and natural animal lover, rose to investigate. We went out to the balcony and flipped on a light.

"Do you see her?" I asked.

Then we both saw her. Directly across, on top of the wall, we could see Burcu, mounted by the big cat while the other cats looked on. There was no way we could get over to where she was, so Osman said we would just have to wait until the owner got back and explain, how his cat was getting raped and all because I'd thought she was a street cat.

The next day, after I got home from work, Osman told me he'd talked to the neighbor, who naturally wasn't very happy about what happened. I asked if they'd managed to rescue Burcu. He said they'd tried, but she didn't want to come back.

At night sometimes I hear her, out in the no-man's land. I've learned to recognize her voice, a shriek, a long, drawn out shriek, like a wild cat. I wonder if the neighbor will take her back, or if she'll just remain with the other cats in the no-man's land, her litter soon to join the others roaming the streets of Kadiköy.

Shoeshine

The *yabancı*, or foreigner, was an American and he had been living in Istanbul for more than two years. He lived with some Turkish university students in an apartment building above the Sedir Cafe in Kadıköy. That morning the American yabancı was heading to catch a shared taxi, or *dolmuş*, to the school in Suadiye where he worked. Spring had arrived just a few days earlier, and it had been an unusually long winter, so he decided to change his routine and head down to the waterfront and walk along the Bosphorous. He spent too much time at the school anyway. It was time to get out and enjoy the new season. He would sit in one of the open cafes on the waterfront and have tea served in the small, hourglass-shaped glasses that Turks said resembled a woman's figure.

Near the busy main intersection he passed a man sitting at one of the benches. He was a shoe-shiner, he had his portable kit with him, and he and the American yabancı made passing eye contact. The American yabancı suddenly remembered he'd been wanting to get his boots shined for several weeks, while the shoe-shiner was already getting off the bench and waving him over.

"*Ne kadar?*" the American yabancı asked, inquiring about the price. The shoe-shiner, who was of indeterminate age – his face seemed young, but scruffy and beat -- seemed not to have heard the question, and continued waving him over.

The American yabancı sat down on the bench and looked down at his boots. He felt much like he did when he finally resigned himself to a haircut. The boots certainly could come in for a polish. They were handsome, black leather Gucci boots that he'd found around Christmas time at one of the small shops near Bahariye Street. He was very proud of them. But now they were dull and scuffed now from the long months of trekking through the city's snow-slushed streets.

The shoe-shiner kneeled and took hold of the American's right boot, lifting it onto a kind of stool attached to the kit. He began applying the black, sludgy polish. The American noticed the man worked with his bare hands, applying the thick gook in swift, crossing movements with his fingers. The forefingers and thumbs were stained black and dirty looking, and he worked quickly. It was a not-unpleasant feeling for the American yabancı, like getting a shave in a barber's shop, where the barber lathers your face with thick soap and applies an old-fashioned blade sharpened on a strap. There was an Old World novelty, like something the American yabancı had seen in black-and-white Hollywood films. He found himself wishing he had a newspaper, or perhaps a cigar, to complete the picture. But not having any of these, he settled for sitting back and watching the shoe-shiner work. The American yabancı's eyes unconsciously passed down to the shoe-shiner's loafers. They looked worn but functional; that is to say, there wasn't anything particularly shiny about them.

The shoe-shiner finished applying the polish to the right boot. He lifted up the lower part of the American yabancı's trousers – the American yabancı wondered how the shoe-shiner managed to avoid getting the polish on his trousers (well, they were black anyway, so it wouldn't matter, he reflected). The shoe-shiner checked to see if the upper part of the boot needed touching up. He made a few passes with his fingertips, then tapped the boot lightly, without looking up, and the American understood that it was time for the left boot.

Gingerly, the shoe-shiner set his right boot down and picked up the left boot onto the stool. The shoe-shiner adjusted the position of the boot, then began applying the polish, using a greasy forefinger and thumb to get at the grooves around the toe and curve of the instep. Shoe-shiner … or would he be called a bootblack? The American yabancı was still enjoying himself with these thoughts. Behind them lay Kadıköy's busy main thoroughfare; the ferry boats in the Bosphorous were running full steam at this time of the morning, carrying students and workers to the European side. The American yabancı thought about the price. The shoe-shiner hadn't said anything and he worried about it a little.He recalled a year or so before in Yeldeğirmeni, an old neighborhood just a few blocks away, paying paying 5 lira, and that man had even taken the American yabancı's shoes off and given him sandals to wear while he went to work on the American yabancı's shoes. He, the yabancı, had been a novelty in Yeldeğirmeni, and the shoe-shiner had brought him tea, and several men from a nearby café had looked on curiously. Five lira then had seemed a reasonable price, and it seemed a reasonable price now.

Just then a young Turk, probably a student, sat down on the bench. The American looked at the young man's shoes. They were black athletic shoes and just needed a quick brush up. He went back to watching the shoe-shiner, who by then had finished applying the polish to his left boot. He was dabbing on now some kind of clear wax, working it with light movements. Then the shoe-shiner put the wax away and produced a tiny whiskbroom that looked like a squirrel's tail, and went to work on the left boot. He moved the brush quickly, in deft, angled movements, coaxing the dull paint into a bright shine. He finished the left boot and, giving the tapping signal, had the American yabancı move it out of the way and bring up the right again.

As he watched the right boot come up for the final shine, the American remembered a portion of Malcolm X's biography he'd read the previous summer, the part where the young Malcolm worked as a shoeshiner at the ballrooms in Boston.You gotta be quick, the other boy tells him. That's the main thing, fast. He teaches young Malcolm how to hustle the white customers, how to size them up and find out how to get them the other, secret things they want. No, the American yabancı thought, remembering the passage more clearly, how to get more money out of them.

Vaguely, the American yabancı wondered if the shoe-shiner had some other hustles. Or maybe he just got by somehow. He remembered a time in Bursa, when the shoe-shiners sat lined up in the streets, and he was on his way to dinner, and one shoe-shiner practically begged him to sit down. When the American yabancı had refused, the next shoe-shiner grabbed him and said, pointing at the first shoe-shiner, "He is my brother! Please!" And the American yabancı had practically had to pry the grip of the second shoe-shiner's fingers from his arm, before he finally escaped. Those shoe-shiners were Kurdish. He wondered if this shoe-shiner was Kurdish. A lot of the people who did the menial work in the city were Kurds.

The shine hadn't taken more than ten minutes. He looked over at the young Turk, who was waiting patiently for his turn. The American wondered if the shoe-shiner mistook him, the yabancı, for a tourist, an out of town businessman. Well, he was a yabancı, an *Ingiliz yabancı* … that's all that mattered. Or did it matter?

The shoe-shiner finished. The American yabancı reached for his wallet, and again asked how much. "Ne kadar?" Again, the shoe-shiner didn't say anything. He sort of dipped his head and made a vague, modest gesture. The smallest bill the American yabancı had in his wallet was a 10-lira note. There were coins, but he didn't want to be stingy. He handed the 10-lira note to the shoe-shiner.

"*Beş lira*," the American yabancı said, showing five fingers. "*Beş.*" He waited for his change.

The shoe-shiner seemed to ignore him, placing the 10-lira note into the shinebox. The young Turk moved over to get his shine, and the bootblack went to work. The American yabancı felt something in him drop and rise at the same time.

He debated, wondering if he should just walk away. It was only 10 lira. Yeah, but 10 lira for a shoe-shine? That seemed too much. Let's wait and see how much the Turk pays, he thought. The shoe-shiner finished shining the shoes of the young Turk, who then bent down and nodded in a polite way, and handed over three, 1-lira coins. "Sağol, abi," the young Turk said, calling the shoe-shiner "brother." In Turkish "brother" is a polite form of address, it doesn't necessarily mean you are related. The young Turk walked briskly away, disappearing round a corner.

The coins flashed gold in the shoe-shiner's dirty hand. He handed them to the American yabancı.

Afterward, he didn't walk down to the waterfront as he'd planned. On the dolmuş to the school, the American yabancı thought about the shoe-shiner, and told himself not to. *Forget about it, he said to himself. OK, so he overcharged you. He could have made even more, but he gave three back. He still came out ahead. Three from the Turk, seven from the yabancı. Really, after two years, you should know how much to pay to have your shoes shined! You should have been firmer at the beginning and insisted on a price before sitting down.* The American yabancı settled on this last thought – any of his students could have told him that – and looked out the window. He put the shoe-shine out of his mind and readied to go to work. The dolmuş by then was coming out past Caddebostan and rounding the coastal road toward Suadiye. The sea shimmered bright in the mid-morning sun. The American yabancı looked down at his boots. They were shining too, almost like new. Really, they looked nice.

Trafik

Metin was a Kurd from the city of Van in Eastern Turkey. He had seven other brothers, and all of them, including Çetin, lived in Istanbul. They shared flats in the same apartment building in Ataşehir, a crowded residential district on the city's Asian side.

The brothers also worked together as drivers for an English school, taking teachers to the companies for lessons. They only had four cars, so they shared the driving duties, a practical strategy since they had to drop off and pick up teachers from morning until evening, from the European side and the Asian side. Depending on the traffic, a commute from one side to the other could four hours or even longer some days, especially if there was an accident on one of the bridges.

On any given day, any of the eight brothers could be on hand, but Metin was the one the American yabancı knew best. He was the one who, upon the American yabancı's arrival in the city two years before, had picked him up at Atatürk International Airport. Metin was standing among all the other people expecting arrivals, and he held a sign with the American yabancı's name high over his head. That first day, as Metin sped round the coastal road from the airport past the remains of the city walls, the Blue Mosque and Aya Sofya, where the American yabancı had his first glimpse of the Bosphorous, the driver Metin had rolled the window down allowing the American yabancı to smoke. It was Metin who had driven him to his first accommodation, a *lojman* for teachers in Ayazağa, and after he transferred to the school in Suadiye, it was Metin who often took him to the company lessons.

Metin was 25, but seemed older, even though he liked to joke around. He was easy-going, well-groomed and funny. Some of the Turks at the school called him, "Gundi," which the American yabancı took to mean silly, but he didn't use this term himself. Often when they drove to the companies, Metin would play Kurdish music on the car stereo – Kurdish traditional music, Kurdish pop – but only when they were alone. If others were in the car, Metin usually kept the stereo turned off. So it was something private they had, the music, which sealed their friendship.

When Metin dropped the American yabancı off at a company, he would always ask, "Kaç saat bitti?" or what time he was finished, and they would arrange for a pick up. The time agreed upon, Metin would make a mark on the schedule he kept on a clipboard in the front seat, and then speed off to pick up the next teacher. On busy days, one of the other brothers would be there when he finished teaching to take him back to the school.

There are many Kurdish people living and working in Istanbul. The Kurds have joined Turks from the Anatolian countryside in migrating from the east to Istanbul in recent decades in search of work and better living conditions. Although Kurdish people do occupy high offices (the majority of AKP representatives, the country's leading political party, are Kurdish, and there are famous singers such as Ibrahim Tatlıses and Hülya Avşar) many of them are poor and not highly educated, so they work menial, relatively unskilled jobs – as waiters and cooks in cafes and restaurants, street cleaners, barbers, and taxi drivers. By comparison, Metin and his brothers had a pretty decent arrangement with the school, even though the hours were long and the work sporadic. During the slow summer season, when most students were on holiday, Metin and his brothers painted houses on the side.

The American yabancı spoke very little Turkish, but when Metin spoke he found they understood each other. Metin graded his Turkish, speaking very simply, as if to a child, so that the American yabancı could follow.

“Istanbul’da trafik çok!” Metin would say, when they were stuck at a busy intersection.

`Evet,” the American yabancı would agree. “Çok traffik!”

“İstanbul çok kalabalık!” Metin would say. Istanbul is too crowded.

“Evet! Çok iş, çok stres.” Too much work, too much stress.

“Iş yok para yok,” Metin would say, continuing their routine. No work, no money. It was like a game of poker.

“Iş yok, kız yok,” the American yabancı would add. No work, no girl.

Metin would laugh.

“Evet, evet,” he said, upping the ante. “Iş yok, aşk yok.” No work, no love.

“Para bitti, hayat bitti,” the American yabancı said, staking higher. “Money finished, life finished.

At this point, the light would change, and the congestion of cars and minibuses and taxis would grind slowly ahead. Metin would signal for a new hand.

“Istanbul’da,” he would say, switching the car into second gear, “İş cok, para yok!” In Instanbul, too much work, no money.

“Evet,” the American yabancı would say, tired of the game. “Van çok güzelmi?” Is Van beautiful?

“Evet, çok güzel.”

“Ne zaman gidiyorsun?” When are you going there?”

“Ağustos. Tatil.” He was going for a holiday in August. They hit another light on Fahrettin Kerim Gökay Caddesi, or Minibus Avenue, as everyone called it, since all the blue minibuses run on the street. It was Thursday, the weekly *bazar*, or street market, was in progress, so traffic was jammed in both directions. At the bazar, people streamed in and out under the tents, browsing over the fresh fruit and vegetables, clothing, knick-knacks. A delivery boy carrying bottled water in huge jugs on the back seat of a motorbike weaved in and out of the traffic, bounced up onto a sidewalk.

Metin and the American yabancı looked on as the delivery disappeared down a side street. "Iyi şoför," Metin said, grinning. Good driver.

The American yabancı looked at the dashboard clock. They had just ten minutes to get to the company in Kozyatağı. Metin noticed the American yabancı looking at the clock and waved him off. He patted the American yabancı's shoulder reassuringly. They would make it on time, don't worry. It was the same as always. Metin changed the conversation:

"Sen? Amerika? Ne zaman gidiyorsun? He wanted to know when the American yabancı was going back to America.

"Bilmiyorum," the American yabancı said. "Belki yaz." He said he didn't know, maybe in summer.

"Amerika çok güzel mi?" Metin asked. America is beautiful?

"Evet, Amerika güzel. Ama, bilmiyorum." Yes, America is beautiful, but I don't know.

Metin smiled. "Turkiye çok güzel mi?"

"Evet. Çok güzel."

The light changed and Metin turned right, getting off the jammed Minibus Street. The going was much smoother, and Metin steered the car skillfully down the narrow streets, slowing to let a garbage collector pass. Another car was approaching from the opposite direction. Metin backed the car up, turning to look over his shoulder. He backed up far enough, stopped and the other car passed. They continued their journey. Metin pointed at the clock. They were very close to the company now and there was five minutes to spare.

"Istanbul çok güzel?" Metin asked. He was still pleased about the time.

"Evet," the American yabancı assented. "Çok güzel ama çok trafik."

"Evet, çok traffik. Çok kalıbalık." It was like a mantra now.

"Evet. Çok iş. Çok stres."

In Istanbul, the *trafik*, the crowds, the work, the stress –are things everyone can agree on. In such a city, with such disparate peoples all jammed together, finding agreement is always a good thing.

25

"Kaç saat biti?" Metin asked, as they pulled up in front of the company. What time do you finish?

"Yedi." At seven.

"Yedi. Tamam. Gürüşürüz. Bye-bye."

On Account

When I first met Bulent, he was working at his brother Edep's shop in Çiçekçi, a pleasant residential area near Uskudar. At the time, I was living in the neighborhood, and the brothers' market stood on corner, and from the top of the hill looking down the street from the market you could see a fine view of the Bosphorous, with all the ships floating in the harbor and out at sea.

Edep was the more outgoing of the two brothers, and he spoke a little bit of English. "I am international!" he would proclaim proudly, when we conversed in halting English. Edep took a liking to me; it was interesting to him that I was American, I suppose. "James, Amerika beautiful?" or he would have me choose: "Amerika? Istanbul? "

Or: "James, Amerika we go," Edep's hands would stretch out in a hypothetically west direction, urging us on. "Amerika big money!"

In contrast, Bulent, the other brother, was reserved, shy. We seldom spoke to one another. His well-combed hair was graying at the temples, though his face was youthful. He seemed so serious all the time.

The two brothers alternated shifts, with one taking the day and the other evenings. They were Kurds from somewhere in the east of Turkey, in the vicinity of Diyarbakır, I gathered, and had come to Istanbul some years ago. Both were married and had children, though I seldom saw them.

I was never good at saving money, and Istanbul is not a cheap city, especially if you like going out a lot, as I did. So usually I found myself broke at the end of every month, with payday still a long week away. Edep was really good about letting me have beer and cigarettes on account. He would keep track of what I owed and I would pay him when I had the money.

Buying on account is actually an old custom in Turkey, going back to the days before credit cards. Shop keepers have what is called the "veresiye defter," or "account notebook," where the names of the regular customers and amounts owed are kept in ink or pencil. Actually in most shops, they don't even use a notebook, just sheets of paper with the names and amounts scratched down in long rows and columns.

Edep was always, as I said, very good about letting me, a yabancı, have beer and cigarettes on account. I probably could have had other things too, like food, but a strange sense of delicacy told me to keep my credit confined to beer and cigarettes. Besides, if I needed to eat there was Fehti at the school who let me have sandwiches on account.

I was shy about asking Bulent. His shy, reserved air had in it something of watchfulness, or so I felt, and indeed when I finally approached him the first time about it he regarded me for a moment, and I saw him consider it, then, with a shy, apologetic smile, he shook his head. It didn't seem like a good idea, or he didn't know me well enough. It was OK, I wasn't surprised. That afternoon I waited until Edep came on for the evening shift, and made sure when I put my beer and cigarettes on the veresiye defter that Bulent was still there, so he could see that Edep knew me and trusted me, that I was a regular customer and that Edep and I already had a sound business arrangement. After that I knew that I probably could have also bought on credit from Bulent, but I still generally preferred to deal with his brother.

A time came, not many months later, when I moved from Çiçekçi back to Kadıköy. The flat was in Yeldeğirmeni, an old quarter of Kadıköy that in

Ottoman times was home to Jewish and Armenian families. Nowadays the neighborhood is a bit rough, and the majority of people who live there are Turks and Kurds.

My first night at the flat, having settled in, I headed out to find the local market. It was on a corner facing an old pizzeria, the kind with the huge brick ovens and from the window you can see the workers shoveling pide and lahmacun in and out of the oven with long, wooden poles. Up the street was the local bakery.

I went into the market and – it was Bulent! He was behind the counter. We both started in surprise, then greeted each other enthusiastically. "Merhaba! Merhaba!" We were actually happy to see each other, to see a familiar face. I asked what he was doing in Yeldeğirmeni and he asked me the same thing. It turns out he was going into business for himself. Edep was fine, he said. He still had the shop in Çiçekçi. That evening I bought a few bottles of Efes and a pack of cigarettes. We shook hands and expressed our surprise again and wished each other good evening.

Outside on the way home I shook my head. Istanbul, a city of 13, 15 million souls. How many markets would that make? And to think of all the markets and all the neighborhoods, that Bulent and I would end up on practically the same street. What were the odds? We took it as a good omen.

Inevitably, it wasn't long before my spending caught up with me, and I was broke again. Putting my head down, I went to see Bulent at the market. I had noticed a change come over him in Yeldeğirmeni. He was a lot more relaxed and outgoing. Maybe having his own shop did that. Our relationship had changed too, and we were much more relaxed around each other.

Anyway, that evening I was broke and when I went to see Bulent, we chatted about the weather, about the neighborhood, about football (he was a Galatasaray fan). I asked if it was OK to have some beer and cigarettes on account, and he said no problem. It was a big relief, and Bulent and it was a good feeling to see that we now had our own arrangement, our own understanding.

I ended up living in Yeldeğirmeni through the summer. It was a long summer, and the days were long and hot. In the evenings I liked to get beer and cigarettes and sit out on the balcony drinking and smoking and watching the planes taking off and arriving at the airport. I tried to guess from the trajectory of the planes where they were headed. Many were headed south, to the pleasure resorts at Bodrum , Antalya and

Marmaris. Others were headed to Europe, to Russia, to points East. Other times I watched the construction of the new metro line near the Nautilus shopping center, or the traffic piled up on the main highway, or the neighborhood women hanging their laundry out to dry on the balconies. It was a great balcony, located in a corner of the building, so that the breezes swirled there and kept the balcony cool even in August and you could see all around the different things happening in the city.

It was a different story down below. Construction crews in the neighborhood had gone to work on the main street, ripping it open to install or replace some pipes underneath. The street stones were piled up alongside the dug-up earth, and all day the sounds of the tractors and the hammers and drills kept the neighborhood very noisy, and the dust was everywhere, mixing with the heat and the noise of the workers. The streets were always crowded with people going to the markets and shops, and you had to step around the work and avoid running into people. In the evenings, it was cooler, the construction workers went home for the day, leaving the tractors parked and silent, and the dust settled. But even in the evenings the smell of the dust stayed in the air, in your nostrils.

“Çok toz!” Bulent would say, when I came in after work. Too much dust. He would complain about how the dust came in during the day and got all over everything in the shop, the fruit, the vegetables, the canned goods, the packets of chewing gum and cigarettes – everything – and he, Bulent, would have to keep everything constantly wiped down with a rag. At one point the work was going on right in front of the shop – the workers ripped up parts of the street in sections – and all day Bulent had to listen to the sounds of the tractors and drills right outside his shop.

I went to the market every evening after work. When I had money I paid in cash, and when I didn’t Bulent let me use the veresiye defter. It was a splendid arrangement, mutually beneficial. Throughout that long, hot, dusty, noisy summer in Yeldeğirmeni I never needed to worry about having ice cold beer and cigarettes to enjoy from my cool balcony high up overlooking the neighborhood. In return, Bulent had a loyal customer, and a fairly large pay out every month. Often my tab would run up into the hundreds, and each month on the tenth I paid the amount in full. “Iyi gün,” the Good Day, we called it.

At the end of the summer, with the new school year starting and autumn on the way, I found that I had to move again. The people I was renting from wanted to rent to the incoming Erasmus students who would pay higher prices. So I found a room in Erenköy, which is quite a ways from Kadıköy. When I moved I still owed Bulent some money, but promised myself I would go and see him as always when I got paid on the tenth.

But in Erenköy I was quickly absorbed by my new surroundings. It's a trim, residential neighborhood, home to fairly well-off professionals and retirees. I fell into a new routine. The flat was very near the school where I worked, and so in the mornings I walked instead of taking the dolmuş. I hardly ever went to Kadıköy anymore except sometimes on the weekends. I even found a local market that let me by on account. I soon forgot all about Yeldeğirmeni and Bulent.

Months passed, a gorgeous Mediterranean fall followed by a pounding, cold winter. For weeks the city was covered in snow and ice. Then I had to move again. This time the flatmate announced, rather abruptly, that he had been offered a position in Barcelona, and was going to move there. After a bit of scrambling, I found a room for rent on Craigslist, and joyfully found myself back once again in Kadıköy.

The first night in the new flat, having paid the first month and deposit, I quickly set my few things in the room and went out for a walk. I walked past the fish markets and the produce markets, the fish and rakı cafes, realizing how much I had missed being in Kadıköy. In comparison, Erenköy was dull, desperate housewife central. Here in Kadıköy was all that I liked about Istanbul, the Bosphorous and the bustle of the crowds on the streets and by the waterfront, all the shops and cafes huddled on busy back streets.

I found myself walking through these back streets, familiarizing myself again with old haunts. Suddenly I was in Yeldeğirmeni, and I knew why I had gone there.

Bulent's eyes widened with surprise and joy when I walked in. "Merhaba! Merhaba!" We shook hands energetically, and I pulled out my wallet. Bulent was already going for the veresiye defter and, taking a pencil from behind his ear, scanned the pages until he found my name. The amount had long ago been added up, months ago, and was waiting to be paid.

After paying the money, I apologized to Bulent for the long delay. I explained, in my halting Turkish, how I had moved to Erenköy, how it was far away, and how I had been busy at work and forgotten. No problem, no problem, Bulent said. He said he had worried that something bad had happened to me, or that maybe I had gone back to America. So we were both relieved, he because the account was settled and I because he had no hard feelings.

It wasn't long before I was back on the veresiye defter with Bulent, even though it was a long walk to his market from my new flat. But when the tenth of the month came, I made sure to head straight over to the market and pay up.

"Iyi gün," I said, handing the money over with a smile. The Good Day.

"Iyi gun," Bulent said, nodding in agreement. "Ben, iyi gün. Sen, kötu gün!" Good Day for me, Bad Day for you.

Later I thought about about Bulent and our agreement. Istanbul is a living body, with a strong heart fed by a vast network of busy veins and arteries. The veresiye defter, even though it is technically illegal these days, is one of the main arteries of commercial life. It is still widely used, especially in the poorer neighborhoods, where people don't have access to credit cards. I doubt the city would ever crack down on the use of the veresiye defter (the reason why it is technically illegal is because the state cannot collect taxes on these hand-to-hand, informal credit transactions). To forbid the use of the veresiye defter would be to clog one of Istanbul's main arteries, the effect could be almost like a cardiac arrest. It would be like cutting off the flow of credit to America; overnight, the great empire would come crashing down. But then, I've always found political analogies to be superficial and weak. I'm just glad that in the end, Bulent and I came out straight.

Trumpet Weather (or, The Music of the Bosphorous)

In the spring and summer I went often to the cafes near the Bosphorous. Every evening there was music. Often it was music from the Black Sea, with its rustic, lively melodies played on the *tulum*, a kind of bag pipe, or on violins and the *saz*, which looks like a guitar with a really thin neck and gourd-like shape, and it produces a bright, oriental sound.

The audience in some cafes got up and danced, holding hands and moving in a circle, executing neat, picturesque footwork from the countryside. They would sometimes dance in circles, a folk dance called the *halay*, and other times it was more like country line dancing, rural, communal, easy to follow.

Other nights there would be a saxophonist, playing "Fly Me To The Moon," with as much strident buoyancy as Sinatra, there on the sidewalk with the ships passing behind him, and his sax case open to receive coins from the passersby. Or there were little gypsy children, with their hand drums and flutes, standing in front of the cafes as near as the waiters would allow them without disturbing the customers. Most of the customers were delighted when the children went into their routine, playing on the drums, one or more of them singing in a childish sing-songy voice the songs of the countryside, accompanied by the flute, and after the song the waiter would let the children approach the tables to collect coins from the tables. The children were very greedy, as young children can be, feeling they have earned their reward, and if you gave them one lira, they would demand two. If you declined, and the waiter started to move them off, the children would hiss at you and unwillingly move away.

One night I even saw a group of Native Americans, though I don't know which tribe they purported to be. They all looked like authentic Indians, and were dressed in feathers and war paint. They played in a style that could be described as Andes Mountain music, with the high flute that sounds like cascading water that I have seen before in traveling shows in California. That night, whoever they were, they drew a big crowd of curious Turks, who only knew of Indians what they had seen in Hollywood films.

In this twilight, musical atmosphere, I found myself withdrawing, drifting. Some nights I played well, other nights not so well, depending on how much I had drunk beforehand to ready myself. But I liked the sound the trumpet made over the sea, carried by the breeze out toward the Blue Mosque. The trumpet, after all, is the voice of empires, of kings, of war and ceremony. I felt that the sound of the trumpet fit Istanbul, an ancient city home to the Romans, the Byzantines and the Ottomans; the trumpet caught its sense of grandeur, its lyrical sweep. Of course, the saz was more subtle, evocative as it is of the Orient, of harem dancers and sultans' robes, but then the trumpet was more heroic, suggestive of battleships in the harbor and raised swords.

There was another reason I saved the majority of my playing for the Bosphorous: my neighbors. At that time I was living in Yeldeğirmeni, and the neighbors were mostly older and conservative, families. On those few occasions when I played at the flat, head-scarved, old women would pass by outside, clicking their tongues in disapproval, while the young children at their side glanced through the window at me, wide-eyed and curious, until the women pulled them away. Later I would get a text message from my flat mate saying that the landlord had called and complained.

All that long summer I continued going down to the waterfront. Sometimes I met other musicians, and sometimes they let me sit with them. But most of them were serious, professional street musicians who were trying to earn their daily bread, and were wary of competition, especially from a yabancı. So I didn't impose, and tried to show my support with a few coins, and just listened to the things they played. Most of the time what they played were Turkish songs, usually folk tunes from Anatolia, the sad, complex Turkish soul coming through the melodies, a Turkish soul that is similar to Arabic but different, for in the melodies one also detects the stray influences, Greek, Bulgarian, European classical …

In the autumn, the great evenings along the Bosphorous began to fade with the light. I went there less and less, having moved to another part of the city, away from Kadıköy, and busy at work. My trumpet went into its case and I rarely took it out.

The winter came. It was a long winter that year, the longest in many years, people said. The snow lay everywhere, in the streets, the rooftops, the sidewalks, for weeks on end, and the winds coming in from the Bosphorous were frozen. Nobody went down to the waterfront now, except a few of the fishermen, and most of the cafes there were closed up. Of course the cold couldn't keep away the hardiest of musicians. They simply moved from the waterfront up to Bahariye Street, where in the evenings the people passed by on their way to the warm restaurants and bars. They could still be found as always, in reliable numbers, on Istikklal Caddesi and Taksim Square, the sound of the music blending with the smoky scent of chestnuts being cooked in the street. Some people gave money, and stopped and listened, but most people were bundled up in jackets and scarves, and passed by in a hurry to get wherever they were going. They bustled by without stopping.

Sometime in March, the long winter ended. Happily and abruptly, it was spring. Warm, Mediterranean breezes again came from the sea, bringing life to the city again. By then, I was back in Kadıköy, and it felt good to be close to the waterfront. It felt good to be outside, and to be able to walk without hurrying, to linger, to go down to the sea and meditate over a cigarette and tea.

One evening, a Sunday, I found myself walking along one of Kadıköy's back streets. It had been a rough weekend, out drinking with friends from the school. I was in a depressed mood; another week gone, another weekend, and nothing much to show for it, not really. It was always that way, or so it seemed. The days turn into weeks, into months and seasons, and before you know it, it's all over.

I wasn't thinking any of these things concretely, they were just sensations. I felt like I was drifting again, desperate, morose, in need of a drink. But I didn't want a drink, not then. I wasn't sure at all what I wanted. I started down one street, changed my mind, turned and went down another before changing my mind again. Where was I going? I didn't know. It was a shame, really, especially since the evening was so pleasant, the weather so ...

Trumpet weather! The phrase popped into my head suddenly. I phrased it again. Trumpet weather. Now that has a nice sound, doesn't it? That's the kind of weather we like, isn't it? And that's what we're going to do. My feeling of emptiness, of depression, melted away as I walked back through the streets toward my flat. I felt a sense of purpose. Around me there were a lot of people out. The Galatasaray match was on and you could hear the roars coming from the TVs in all of the bars.

Back at the flat, it was dark inside. Nobody was home. I went to my room and took the trumpet out of its case. I gave it a quick rub, and checked the valves, adding a bit of oil. I blew into the mouthpiece, registering the warm air passing through the bell. *Trumpet weather*! It was ready to go.

Outside, I passed the fish and raki bars, which were full of people watching the match, and the roars of the crowds echoed through the streets. A waiter who knew me wished me good evening. “Iyi akşamlar!” He wanted to know if I was going to watch the match; he waved happily to an empty place at one of the tables. I wished him good evening and went on.

Around the corner, you could see the sun beginning to set over the waterfront. Another twenty minutes and it would be dark. Or maybe thirty minutes, if we could get there in a hurry. I gripped my trumpet case and walked faster.

The Burning of Haydarpaşa

The American yabancı was sitting in a bar in Üsküdar. The bar was tucked away on a back street a few blocks away from the busy main thoroughfare that leads down to the ferry boat station. Üsküdar is a conservative district of Istanbul. Most of the women are covered, and there aren't many bars. Up on the hills away from the busy main street are wonderful examples of old Ottoman houses.

Finding the bar had been a surprise for the American yabancı, for as far as he could tell, it was the only bar in the area. He'd found it by chance during his wanderings of the back streets one weekend. Inside, the bar was gloomy and depressing. All of the customers were men, and most of them were old. They sat over glasses of beer or rakı and watched the horse races on TV, and the football matches in the evenings. The local favorite team was Beşiktaş, eight minutes away on the ferryboat.

On the wall near the TV was a painting of an old drunkard, his face corpuscular, puffy, the nose red with burst capillaries, and he is grinning in a half-absent, half-tipsy like an errant schoolboy, his eyes are rolling, mischievous. The American yabancı, when he drank his beer, tried not to look at the painting.

He didn't go to the bar that often, preferring the livelier places in Kadıköy. But he liked the feeling of being hidden away from the world that the bar in Üsküdar offered. No one could find or disturb him there. He would usually take along his notebook and work on a story, and the other customers left him alone. There were always the same two waiters working. One's name was Servet, and the other was Çağdaş. Both were in their early twenties and were from Istanbul.

Çağdaş was very keen on learning English, and said he wanted to go to America. He treated the American yabancı with great respect, like an old buddy, and always wanted to try out his English with the American. Servet, in contrast, could care less where the American yabancı came from, and had no interest in visiting America, but he saw that the American yabancı was a semi-regular customer who tipped fairly well, and so he was always courteous. He promptly refilled the American yabancı's glass when he saw it was empty, cleaned the ashtray, and set a plate of peanuts or olives on the table free of charge.

One weekend in late November, the American yabancı was at the bar in Üsküdar, sipping beer and scrawling some notes for a story. It was a story about a conservative Muslim girl who by night performs a strip show for an online sex website. İt was a juicy story and he was enjoying writing it. Something on the TV caught his attention. It was turned to CNN Turk and a big fire was in progress. The story was developing.

The American yabancı could tell from the TV images that the fire was at Haydarpaşa, the big, old, famous train station that stood overlooking the Bosphorous. The ferry boats crossing from the European side of the city always stopped to drop off passengers there.

The fire was on the roof, or so the American yabancı surmised. Thick black smoke poured from the roof down into the Bosphorous. It had rained earlier, and the skies were still grey, so the thick black smoke made the sky even darker, plunging the city into a premature night. Fire crews were working from boats, aiming their hoses up toward the roof, but the building was too tall for the hose spray to reach. The spray travelled in a puny parabola, falling pitifully short of the mark.

Çağdaş was working that afternoon; Servet wasn't coming in until later. There were hardly any customers at all, so Çağdaş occupied himself by wiping down tables, and occasionally going to the doorway to look out and scan the street. When Çağdaş passed him, the American yabancı directed his attention to the TV.

"Evet. Çok kötu." Cağdaş said. Yes, it was very bad. He shook his head and kept watching, then went to turn up the volume. The sound of the Turkish broadcaster's voice flooded into the deserted bar.

An old man, bald, with a trim grey mustache, was reading a newspaper at the next table. When the volume went up, he put down the paper and, removing his glasses, peered at the TV. His eyes were black and shiny, fixed on the screen.

The American yabancı was curious to see the old man's reaction. Haydar Paşa was an historic landmark, after all. The man's face didn't register any visible emotion. When the American yabancı addressed him with a remark, the man turned and faced him but seemed not to have heard or understood. But momentarily, something registered in his face. "Evet. Çok kötu," repeating what Çağdaş had just said. Yes, it was very bad.

On the TV, the old train station continued to burn, at least from the top, and the smoke grew thicker, reaching over the waters of the Bosphorous to Eminönu and Sultanahmet, giving the city an apocalyptic visage, as if the city were being bombarded. The fire crews continued to try and direct the hoses at the roof; it appeared the spray was getting a little closer now to the roof, but not much.

"Why don't they try dropping water from a helicopter or plane?" The American tried pantomiming this idea to the old man, and to Çağdaş up at the bar. They both nodded in agreement, but then shrugged and continued watching the TV and listening the journalist.

The American yabancı ordered another beer. "Pesevenk," Cağdaş said, setting the beer down. He was referring to the TV. Çağdaş even turned to the old man and repeated it, and the old man seemed to agree and added something more. The American yabancı knew what pesevenk meant, " pimp." He wondered if Çağdaş was directing the insult at the firemen, and their lackluster efforts. Then he guessed correctly that he meant the insult for whoever had started the fire.

Çağdaş confirmed this guess a few minutes later. "They want," said Çağdaş, struggling to formulate his ideas into English. "They want – they want, make big shopping center." He pointed again at the screen, and gesticulated wildly, shaking his fist at the TV. The old man was more sedate, but he nodded in agreement. "Çok pesevenk!" Çağdaş said, snapping his cloth at a table dismissively.

Ah, so that was it. The American yabancı thought he understood now, and sipped his beer. The American considered the theory, reflecting on what his students had told him, and what he had read in the English media, of Istanbul's building boom, of the shady politics surrounding the building industry. It certainly seemed possible. He thought about how grand and elegant the Haydarpaşa train station looked, at the water's edge, when you passed it on a ferry.

Come to think of it – what was he doing, sitting there at the bar? Only a few years before, working at the newspaper in California, he had covered fires before. He remembered the great summer fires in Legget and Gasquet, the fires that had spread over many miles, devouring forests and homes, and even threatening towns, while all the people packed and fled to escape the approaching fires. He remembered jumping into a car with the photographer and racing to the perimeter, as close as the fire crews allowed the journalists to come. He remembered interviewing firefighters, and fleeing families, the fire so close your could smell the smoke, your eyes stung with it, and the heat was nearly unbearable. Some days they had driven as many as 50 miles to report on the summer fires.

And now here he was, the American yabanı thought, in Istanbul, with Haydarpaşa burning, not 20 minutes away. He could get a dolmuş and be there in 20 minutes, maybe even sooner. But he would have to stop by his flat and get his camera. But that was on the way. Total time, he could be there in half an hour. He felt something of the old excitement on the tip of his tongue.

But it could be all over by then. Probably. Besides, he thought, CNN's already got the story. The Turkish press for sure has it. What would he do with the story even if he had it? Who could he sell it to? If CNN had it, then anybody who cared to pick it up already had it. There were probably twenty journalists there already.

The American yabancı finished his beer, and looked over at the old man. The old man had gone back to reading his newspaper, with his glasses on. Çağdaş was already bringing another beer to the American yabancı's table. "Çok kötu," he said again, looking at the fire one more time and shaking his head. Very bad. Then he flipped the channel. A football match was getting ready to start. Çağdaş turned the volume up so you could hear the roar of the crowd.

The American yabancı went back to looking at his notes for the story about the Muslim girl, the young girl who was covered by day and who was a webcam stripper by night. He looked over what he had written, and sipped his beer, trying to keep the sound of the roaring football fans, and everything else, out of his mind.

***Author's note:** The fire was brought under control and extinguished later that same evening. News reports later determined the cause of the fire to be carelessness. In January 2012, Today's Zaman reported that the train station would be renovated and transformed into a cultural center.

Bride in the Dusk, Thief in the Night

Istanbul is a city that is best seen from the Bosphorous at dusk, so if you ever get invited for an evening boat cruise, jump at the chance. My chance came in the form of a wedding. Our neighbor, Osman, who sells bottled water in a small shop next to our flat, invited us recently to the wedding of his son, Fatih.

The ceremony was in the municipal building in Kadiköy, a relatively short ceremony, since it being mid-summer, the building was booked all day long by different parties.

The bride and groom had booked a ferry for the reception. For a while my flat mates and I had debated going; we had dinner and a few beers at a restaurant near the fish markets. But then Osman's phone rang. It was Osman. Where were we? They were waiting for us! We ran down to the waterfront and caught the ferry just minutes before it left the pier.

What followed was a rare, magic evening on the Bosphorous. It had been hot all afternoon, but on the boat it was mild and breezy, and as evening came on the waters churned behind us like silver flying fish.

We met the bride and groom. The bride Ayşe wore a cream-colored silk dress that trailed like a cloud behind her, and her dark, Gypsy-like features had the glow of happiness as she greeted the guests. The groom, Fatih, wore a white tuxedo and his longish hair was swept back over his high forehead. We knew him from the neighborhood; his father owned a small shop that sold bottled water to the people who lived in the nearby apartments. That afternoon took Osman and me in hand and led us in the *halay*, a festive, Black Sea dance in time to the music, and soon he grabbed up other guests and everyone was dancing.

Other boat parties passed and we waved to them and they waved back. We went around the Golden Horn , past the Aya Sofia and the two bridges and went all the way to Uskudar, past the bluish, ghostly mosque at Ortaköy, a trip of some three hours.

There was more dancing, with the bride and groom linking arms with the other guests and dancing in circles around the deck. The more conservative women in their *çarşaf*, a kind of Arabic head-covering that Turks called "bed-sheet," as well as the normal headscarves, sipped juice or water and happily looked upon the festivities. The children, delighting in the mysteries of the boat and in the fact that the adults were busy, took to playing spy hunt and hide and seek on the lower decks. For Osman and I, the absence of alcohol became more painfully apparent (this was a more conservative Muslim family), but we'd tanked up a bit beforehand, and really we didn't miss it so much.

As it got even later, the music pumping from the speakers, traditional Turkish as well as modern Turkish pop and techno, beat steadily on and the dancing increased; we danced and danced all the way back, as if to savor the evening and its possibilities to their fullest before having to return to port and reconnect with the world, its more mundane journeys, to home and to work, to Monday morning.

We got off the boat in Kadıköy feeling flushed and happy, as if we had just got married ourselves, only the bride was the city itself, looking resplendent under the stars.

The following Friday I returned to my flat. It was Friday, and I was looking forward to the weekend. To Osman, my flatmate, I suggested we go out for something to eat, then went to my room to retrieve some cash. But when I checked the envelope where I had the money hidden, about 1,000 lira – the money was gone! And I'd just checked the money that morning.

We summoned the police. Two detectives showed up and dusted for fingerprints and interviewed Osman and Yusuf, our other flatmate. Our initial feelings, mine anyway, was that someone had come through the window, since my windows were open. But we live on the third floor, and it's a good ten, 12 meters down to the garden.

The police didn't believe my story, Osman said. They thought I was just making the whole story up about the missing 1,000. That made me even angrier – as if I

enjoy having detectives in my flat on a Friday evening!
The detectives left and three uniformed officers came. One of them was a young woman, attractive and serious.
"Do you speak English?" she asked me, after taking a look in my room. I got angry with the policewoman too, for she had smiled while I was telling what happened in a way that infuriated me, as if she seemed satisfied with my misfortune.
"This is funny for you!" I said.
"No, it's not," she said. "But this is Istanbul! Thieves are everywhere. This is the second call like this for me tonight. It doesn't matter you live on the third floor, they can climb ninth floor."
Osman and I went with the police to the precinct office, near the dolmuş station. By then it was after midnight. The interior of the office was lit with the harsh, antiseptic light of police stations the world over. We were told to wait on a bench while the police officers disappeared into another office. Meanwhile, two tarts, one of whom Osman insisted was a drag queen, sat on a nearby bench eyeing us and laughing. The sight of these two whores, combined with the late hour, the sickly light of the precinct, was infuriating.
"Why don't you go and suck a cock?" I shouted, not caring if they understood English or not.
A middle-aged cop suddenly yelled in our direction. "*Gel! Gel!*" "Come! Come!" He said, not bothering with the formal tense, speaking as if to dogs. I have never seen such swarthy, piggish hate in a policeman's eyes. He waved his arms rudely, clearly showing his disgust.

We were ushered into the smaller office, where the young policewoman now sat behind a computer. I was still far from calm, but actually the policewoman, who Osman later told me was named Berna, was quite professional and not unattractive. In fact, she seemed sympathetic and interested in us – which may have explained the hate in the older cop's eyes, the bastard was jealous. Over the next hour or so, Berna went over our statements, typed them up, and we signed them. By the time we finally left, it was after two.

"So now you know this is Istanbul ," Berna said. "Be careful."

"This a normal day for you?" I asked, still unable to let it rest. "Well, if so, you take care of yourself."

She couldn't resist laughing, a pleasant, girlish laugh. "*You* take care of *your*self, James!"

We left, and walked back to the flat. On the way, we stopped at the shop to pick up a few beers, consolation for a Friday night lost. Yavus was working, and when he heard about what happened, gave me the beers, and a pack of cigarettes, on credit, and we got kebab sandwiches to take back to the flat.

Back home, we went over everything again. Fortunately (and interestingly), the thief had not taken my passport or visa, which were located in the same place as the cash. That's one of the reasons the police didn't believe my story – passports and visas would have been stolen by a "professional thief," as there is a lucrative black market. Also, as I learned later from other colleagues, an Istanbul thief goes through everything, overturning desks, mattresses, scattering papers. My room had been essentially untouched: just the cash was missing. So the deduction was: I was either lying, or the thief had been someone who lived in the flat. That would mean Osman or Yusuf. It was hard to suspect Osman: after all it had been he who accompanied me to the police station. Yusuf I suspected, for just a few days before he had told Osman he was broke and was maybe going to move out. Also, with my windows open he could easily have come through from his balcony. Osman had been painting one of the rooms and said he didn't hear anything. Yusuf claimed he and his girlfriend Hülya had been out swimming all day.

The next evening, Osman hatched a plan: he would call up Yusuf and Hülya and say that we had interviewed the neighbors and that one of them had seen them in the room taking my money. Ideally, if they were guilty, they would wilt and confess once confronted with the prospect of an eyewitness.

It was a plausible plan, but it made me uneasy. I'm always a bit squeamish about using such manipulative tactics. It seemed to me that its success was predicated on the assumption that they were 100 percent guilty, and I wasn't sure they were. But as Osman pointed out, it was more like a test. Afterward, we could apologize and say we were just testing them to be sure. Still, I was nervous. It seemed too easy and obvious; after all, the thing about cash is it's clean, untraceable. If Yusuf or his girlfriend had stolen the money, and were sure of themselves, and that the money could not be traced, then all they had to do was just hold their ground and call our bluff. After all, we could not prove anything.

“Come on, man!” Osman said, after listening. “It was Yusuf! You know it! I know it!” He chided me for my squeamishness. He said if I didn’t want to do it, then I must be lying about the whole thing to begin with. I argued back, why would I steal from myself?

Finally, thinking that perhaps he was right, I yielded to Osman’s detective tactics. He made the calls to Yusuf and Hülya. We figured if they were guilty they would put off coming to the flat, that maybe we would in fact not see them again.

Actually Hülya arrived fairly quickly, an attractive, spirited young girl. I’d overheard her arguments with Yusuf, and always felt sorry for him, for she had the kind of shrill voice that always prevails over reason, even her own. So you understand I was not looking forward to any kind of confrontation.

They preferred to talk about it in Turkish, so they kept me out of the discussion, even when Yusuf arrived later. It was better actually, I thought, to let the Turks work it out between themselves.

Our great scheme to “trap” them fell flat on its face. Hülya, innocent or guilty, was clever and kept her poise. She immediately inquired who it was that allegedly saw them in the room. Osman, who perhaps had anticipated this, went downstairs. While he was gone, Hülya went to her Facebook account and opened up a photograph of another girl, one of her friends.

In a few minutes, Osman returned with the wife of the family downstairs (we’d danced at the wedding the weekend before). She greeted everyone pleasantly, and I realized that Osman had in desperation just gone and hastily briefed her on the situation and she'd amiably agreed to help us.

But Hülya was ready. She asked our would-be witness to look at the photograph of her friend on the Facebook page. Did she look like that, Hülya asked? Yes, our witness said, nodding. Hülya turned to us, a look of triumph flashed in her eyes. "You see! My friend has blonde hair, I have dark! We do not even look the same!"

All the evening produced was: they said they would move out at the end of the month.

The following evening, Sunday, Osman went out with his friends. I'd decided to let the whole go and try to salvage some remnants of the weekend. It was a warm, windy evening. Yavus gave me a few beers on credit, and I watched a film, an old favorite," Manhattan." Later, I went to bed but I couldn't sleep. It was hot, a slight breeze blowing in. But I wasn't comfortable having the windows open. I got up and shut them and closed the curtain. But that made sleep even harder, so I got up and opened the windows again. Later Yusuf came out on the balcony and we talked for awhile. I was a bit drunk and so less guarded than the day before. "*I know it was you,*" I said sententiously. "*It was you, Yusuf.*" I said this over and over.

Yusuf took it surprisingly well.

"Man, are you drunk?" he asked. "If I need money, my family can help me. Here in my room, I have a computer, a camera, if I need money I can sell them.

Tomorrow I am going to maybe start new work in Taksim. Have you thought about Osman? Yes? You know where does he get his money? From us! We pay for this flat. I think it was Osman who took your money."

It was dark and the lights of the other flats across the garden were on; a couple of girls from the student building came out, then went back in. I went to bed. It was still hard to sleep in the heat, the stultified air. There was still much good here, trying to sleep in the heat, the stultified air. There was the wedding, for example, when on that ferry cruising up the Bosphorous, it seemed Istanbul itself were a bride, and you and the city itself were joined in matrimony. Perhaps, for me anyway, that is Istanbul: it is both a bride in the dusk, and a thief in the night.

The Trumpet Fisherman

It was usually late afternoon or early evening when The old man Galip took his trumpet out. The sound of the waves breaking against the rocks accompanied the busy hum of the harbor and passing ships.

The old man Galip walked with the trumpet case in hand, swinging loosely at his side. He was very thin but solidly built, a wiry seventy, and his grey hair was combed carefully. His clothes were simple, a white shirt and black trousers, loafers that he kept shined regularly.

There were always many people out, so he scanned along the long line of rocks for a relatively isolated spot. Here and there were uniformed policemen, but they didn't appear too bothered about anything. They walked in twos and threes up and down the boardwalk.

It was a little bit like fishing, the old man Galip thought: Choosing the right spot. When he was a boy in Üsküdar he had often gone with his father, but he himself had never been good at it, and had become a musician instead.

Still he often liked to watch the fishermen who came out to fish on the rocks, there in Kadıköy but also in Üsküdar, the Galata Bridge over on the European side, at Bostancı, and all along the Bosphorous. The old man Galip knew they fished primarily for *hamsi*, the little fish that are like anchovies, and taste wonderful fried up and served with rakı. His wife had used to make it for him on Sunday afternoons, but she had died three years before. He was staying now with one of his daughters, Selma, but she and her husband were very busy with their work and so now when he wanted hamsi and rakı the old man Galip usually prepared it himself, or went to one of the places in Kadıköy.

There were always many fishermen along the Bosphorous, and The old man Galip always wondered, with so many fishermen, how they ever managed to catch anything. But for most of them the fishing was primarily for sport, he presumed. He thought of his old friend Ali used to go out every weekend before a second heart attack confined him to the home. He visited his friend usually in the mornings, they had tea and read the newspapers together.

The old man thought about getting some fish for Ali. He would have to remember the next time he went to the fish market in Kadıköy.

Reaching the wide open section of the boardwalk, where you can see directly across to the Aya Sofya and Blue Mosque, and the sea wall cuts in a long, flat line, protecting the harbor from the open sea, The old man Galip could see it was very crowded. It was still very light out. He would have to walk further down, towards Moda.

So he kept walking. Gypsy women were selling flowers and bottled water, and a man was selling simit. The old man Galip passed by the sellers, scanning the rocks. There were people everywhere, mostly young people but really people of all different ages. An old woman was being pushed in a wheelchair. She looked absently out at the sea, her withered face pale and exposed in the sun, while a young man pushed the chair. I'll have to remember to play something for her, The old man Galip thought.

Walking further down, he saw that it wasn't going to get any better, no matter how far he walked. And he was getting tired of walking besides. He was anxious to get the trumpet out while the light was fine; on the Bosphorous it could change so quickly. That was another part he liked, checking the light, and again for some reason he was reminded of fishing.

The spot he finally settled on was as good as any. It was a kind of tiny alcove, a break in the rocks, down near the waterline looking out at the sea rather than the Bosphorous. He climbed down, careful not to slip. His daughter Selma didn't like him coming out and always worried about him falling on the rocks.

He felt the wind stronger the closer he got to the water. Here the waves came in and landed but not too hard. Surveying the waves, the old man Galip gauged the power of the waves, seeing how high the waves swelled when they reached back and came forward. It was best not to get too close.

The old man Galip sat on a rock that was flat like a chair, leaning back against another rock, and set his case down. Once, the previous summer he had been careless; the case had slipped on the rock and tumbled down into the water and he had just caught it in time. It would be a hell of a way to lose a trumpet, he thought, remembering.

Now, the case safely tucked away, The old man Galip opened the case. The trumpet shined in the sunlight. He took it out and put some oil into the valves, blew into the mouthpiece and checked the air flow. The bell was cold, and he continued to blow air, hoping to warm it up. But it was still early spring and the air was chilly and damp, despite the sun.

The first notes came out sputteringly, weak. He took a deep breath, wiped his lips, adjusted his embouchure, and tried again. A solid middle 'G' rang out over the sea. The old man Galip went up to a 'C', hit it, and down to a low 'C.' Then he ran through a series of scales, not playing them in the cycle as he should, but randomly.
He definitely had fallen off with the long winter break. The trumpet, having been stuck in its case all through the cold months, now seemed obstinate, spiteful. It failed to obey his commands, or rather, went through the motions coldly, with resistance. The old man Galip could already feel the muscles around his lips straining; it would take a while to get them back into playing shape.

The old man Galip ran through a few minor scales, and then, touched the bell again. It was still cold. It was the weather, he thought. In June, July it won't take any time at all to warm it up. The thing to do was to take it easy. *Remember,* he thought to himself, *you are not here to give a concert. You don't have to dazzle anybody. That's not why you are here. Just play. Inşallah.*

The old man Galip went into something he remembered from "Porgy and Bess," a bittersweet tune, "Bess, You Is My Woman Now," playing just the chorus. The trumpet was still obstinate, making him pay for the rust, but gradually the trumpet gave itself over to the joyous melody.

The old man Galip knew that a few of the people nearby were watching him, listening, but he made no effort to acknowledge them. Two young schoolgirls, wearing their *lycee* uniforms, sat directly behind him, and he could feel their eyes looking at him, but he just played. He knew that he wasn't playing very well, that his wind wasn't strong from the diaphragm (he really needed to cut down on smoking, he thought for the thousandth time) and he could not sustain the notes the way he wanted. But it was early season; those things would come back, as long as he kept at it. They always came back.

He went into a few other songs, "My Way," and a few phrases from a Count Basie blues number he had used to like. His father had loved American jazz and popular music. Sinatra had been his idol. He thought about his father as he played.

Again, there was hesitation, missed notes; he realized he'd forgotten the fingering, but he struggled with it nevertheless, listening as the melody shakily came together and he finally got it. Let them have that one, The old man Galip let himself smile with satisfaction. *It doesn't matter anyway, remember? All these notes, whatever you play or how you play them, it all goes into the sea. The sea takes them all, the good notes and the bad. Inşallah.*

He was pleased with this last thought, the idea of the sea rushing in with its power and vast forgetfulness, washing away all things, and bringing in new things too. And the other people who came out, old woman in her wheelchair, the two young girls sitting behind him, or the people sitting higher up on his right. They went there for different reasons perhaps, but maybe they too had something they wanted to wash away, or to receive something of the sea's message.

He played something Turkish, the first phrases of a popular song called, "Sensiz Olmaz," or ~Without You," in the melancholy, melismatic Turkish style. But he realized he was bored of that song, he had played it all last summer. He really needed to learn some other Turkish songs. Friends had suggested he learn something from Turkan, as well as Sezin Aksul, two of the country's most popular singers at the moment. He had heard one of Sezen Aksu's sad melodies about her beloved Aegean, and he had told himself to learn the melody. But at the moment, he could not summon it in his memory.

Just then a young man came and tapped his shoulder. He introduced himself as Zafer, and pointed to a group of young men who were playing together about 50 meters further down. They had guitars and were singing in merry voices.

"Are you a professional, *baba*?" Zafer asked. "Can you play any other new Turkish songs? Tarkan? You must know Tarkan! You must know this one!"

Zafer began singing the melody of the Turkan song, trying to jog his memory. The old man Galip obligingly made efforts to mimick the melodies, with varying degrees of success. He tried to explain to the young Turk that he had only come out to practice. He waved to the other musicians they waved back. Their playing was very faint under the sounds of the sea.

Zafer left finally, with a disappointed air, promising they would see each other again. The old man Galip felt embarrassed somehow by the encounter, probably because he had tried to play the Turkish songs, for showing his ignorance of the new music, his rust.

It was still light out, but the sun had gone behind some clouds, and it was getting chilly. Suddenly the imam could be heard from a distant loudspeaker. The afternoon prayer.

The old man Galip quietly listened to the imam, and when the prayer was done, he decided to pack up. The two young women behind him were gone. They had left sometime while he was playing with Zafer and he found he wished they had stayed.

Walking back along the boardwalk, The old man Galip could feel the effects of the playing. The muscles around his mouth were a little sore, but he felt stronger, refreshed, from the walk and from the playing. Actually he felt tired all over. He would have to have a glass of tea and a bath when he got home, and Selma would be asking where he had been.

When he passed one of the gypsy women selling water, he stopped and bought a bottle for 1 lira. The gypsy woman thanked him and wished him well.

The old man Galip felt better. The gypsy woman seemed to treat him with respect, knowing he had not had a great day, but understanding there were reasons. He felt like a fisherman again, a trumpet fisherman. Today had not been a successful day. He had not had a big catch. But sometimes it was like that. Sometimes the fishermen might be out there all day and, casting their poles into the sea, not catch a single fish. Maybe it depended on the mood of the sea as much as the ability of the fisherman. Today the sea would not give him the warm air to keep his horn warm for the melodies to come through. Perhaps it would tomorrow. He would just have to keep coming back, and remember to practice the Turkish melodies. There were always new songs to learn.

He thought again about the night last summer when he had stayed out really late, after almost everyone else had gone, and the waters of the sea were oily black, shiny in the moonlight. He had stayed out and played, and he had played very well, the notes carrying the full, bright ripple that he knew they should have, and at a certain point a couple of dolphins had come up splashing. They were there for just a single instant, and you heard them more than actually saw them, just the round shiny heads emerging for a moment before disappearing with a flick of the tail. But they had been there, and The old man Galip had wondered if the dolphins were attracted, with their deep-sea, millennial intelligence, by something they heard in what he played, and he wondered if he could ever do it again, *to play so as to attract the fish from the sea.* He would truly be a trumpet fisherman then, if he could do it again. He would try, The old man Galip thought to himself. Yes, he would go back and keep trying. *Inşallah.*

www.ingramcontent.com/pod-product-compliance
Ingram Content Group UK Ltd.
Pitfield, Milton Keynes, MK11 3LW, UK
UKHW041919190726
13854UKWH00003B/1321

9 781105 644375